I0884300

TABLE OF CONTENTS

Getting an Idea on Paper

Every book starts the same way. A curious person has an idea or question. What if frogs could fly? What if the dog could talk? Where do armadillos live?

Authors write down their ideas. They research facts. Artists might sketch a character. They create. They change their minds. They write or draw some more. This process may take a year or more. But that is just the beginning!

Author writes a story.

MONTH 1

. . . LOADING . . . LOADING . . .

MAKING A BOOK

BY NADIA HIGGINS

SEQUENCE

AMICUS | AMICUS INK

Sequence is published by Amicus and Amicus Ink
P.O. Box 1329, Mankato, MN 56002
www.amicuspublishing.us

Cataloging-in-Publication data is available from the Library of Congress.
LCCN: 2017049060
ISBN 978-1-68151-440-6 (library bound)
ISBN 978-1-68152-360-6 (paperback)
ISBN 978-1-68151-522-9 (ebook)

Editor: Wendy Dieker
Book Designers: Ciara Beitlich and Veronica Scott
Photo Researcher: Holly Young

Photo Credits: Vtmila/Shutterstock cover; wavebreakmedia/Shutterstock 5; GaudiLab/Shutterstock 6; Pixsooz/iStock 8–9; baranq/Shutterstock 10; Aila Images/Shutterstock 12–13; Jeffrey G. Kirkpatrick/Alamy 14; Wavebreakmedia Ltd/Dreamstime 16–17; Hero Images/Getty 19; Alissa Kumarova/Shutterstock 20–21; zefart/Shutterstock 22, 24–25; zefart/iStock 26; kali9/iStock 29

Printed in China

HC 10 9 8 7 6 5 4 3 2 1
PB 10 9 8 7 6 5 4 3 2 1

Anyone can come up with an idea for a book. What ideas do you have?

OADING . . . LOADING . . . LOADING . . .

An agent works hard to contact publishers for authors.

Author writes a story.

MONTH 1 MONTH 2 ...DING . . . LOADING . .

Author lands an agent.

The next step is finding a **publisher** to buy the story. A publisher is in the business of making books. But publishers are busy. Most of them will not even read an author's work unless they know the author already. So authors need **agents** to help. Finding an agent is a huge break. The agent sends the story to publishers.

OADING . . . LOADING . . . LOADING . . .

Now the **editor** takes over. This person is an expert reader. They will see what they think of the story. Does it give them chills? Does it make them laugh out loud? Are they sad when they have to put it down? Yes! The story is accepted. The publisher agrees to buy the story. It will become a real book!

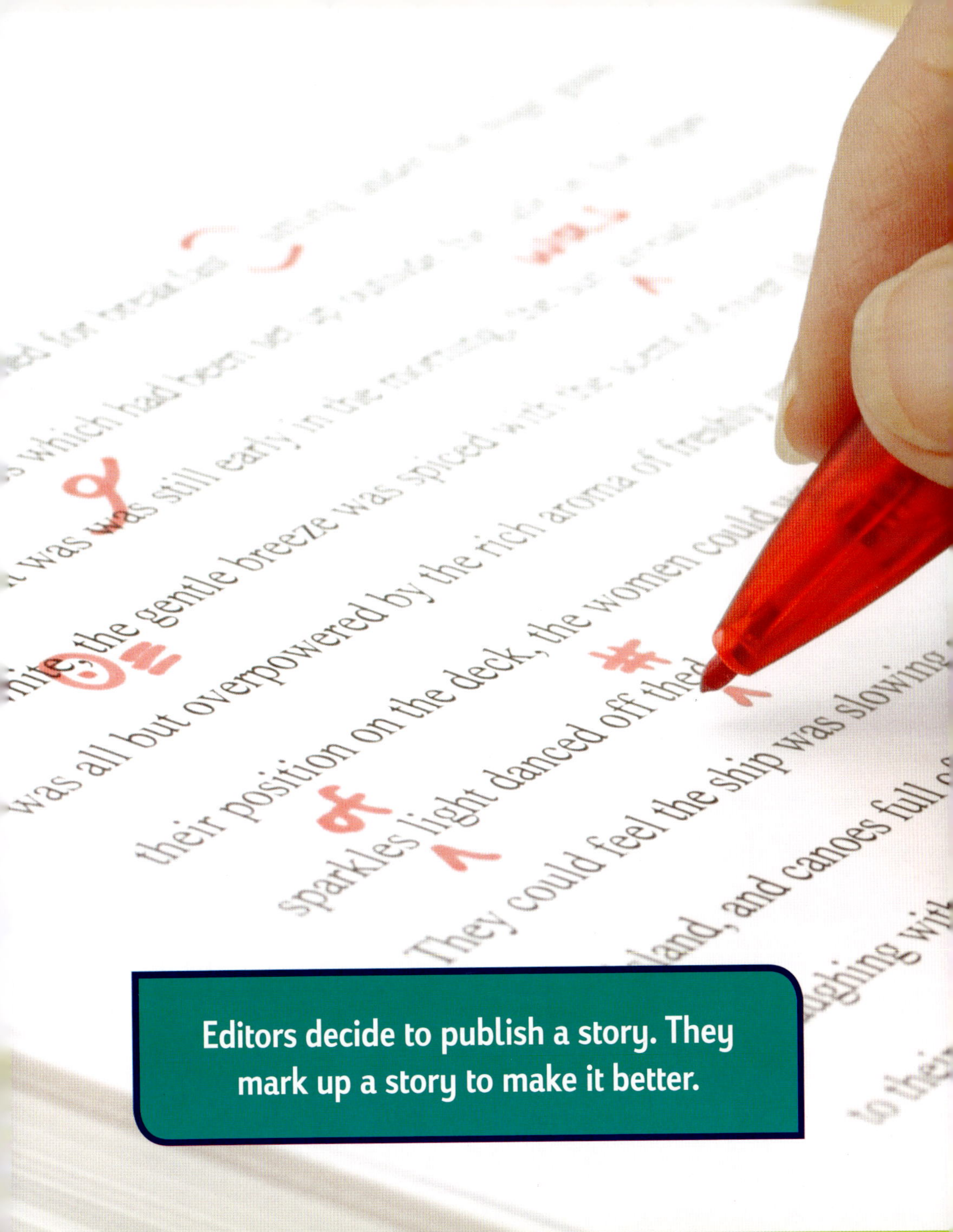

Editors decide to publish a story. They mark up a story to make it better.

A team of people work on ideas to make a story really great.

Author writes a story.

MONTH 1

Author lands an agent.

MONTH 2

Book is accepted for publication.

MONTH 6

Author and editor revise story.

MONTH 7

OADING . .

It Takes a Team

Dozens of people work together to make a book. The editor is in charge of the **text**. An editor may have big ideas for making the story even better. He sends notes to the author. *Add another character. Change the ending. Move this part to the end.* The story goes through more **drafts**.

LOADING . . . LOADING . . . LOADING . . .

Another editor is thinking about the book itself. What size will it be? Will there be an e-book? These decisions affect the how much it will cost to make the book.

The **publicist** is brainstorming, too. How will they get this book noticed? With ads? A website? Should the author do a book tour? The publicist makes a plan.

A publicist comes up with a plan to spread the word about the book.

- MONTH 1: Author writes a story.
- MONTH 2: Author lands an agent.
- MONTH 6: Book is accepted for publication.
- MONTH 7: Author and editor revise story.
- MONTH 8: Book cost is set; publicity decisions are made.

LOADING . . . LOADING . . . LOADING . . .

- MONTH 1: Author writes a story.
- MONTH 2: Author lands an agent.
- MONTH 6: Book is accepted for publication.
- MONTH 7: Author and editor revise story.
- MONTH 8: Book cost is set; publicity decisions are made.
- MONTH 12: Illustrator and designer work on the layout.

Finally, the story is set. The **illustrator** can get to work. This artist reads the book many times. What parts will make the best pictures? The illustrator draws some pencil sketches.

The **designer** is working out the book's **layout**. Will the words be on the same page as the pictures? How big should the words be? What color?

An artist draws pencil sketches for a book before adding color.

Designers create many drafts of a book cover. The team wants the best cover possible.

- MONTH 1: Author writes a story.
- MONTH 2: Author lands an agent.
- MONTH 6: Book is accepted for publication.
- MONTH 7: Author and editor revise story.
- MONTH 8: Book cost is set; publicity decisions are made.
- MONTH 12: Illustrator and designer work on the layout.

The designer is worried about the book's cover. It has to be good. The cover needs to grab the readers. It needs to stick in their minds.

The design team may come up with 10 cover choices. Everybody weighs in. Will there be a winner? If not, it's back to the drawing board.

MONTH 13 LOADING . . . LOADING . . .

A cover design is chosen.

Putting It All Together

The text is ready. The sketches are in. The layout is done. How does everything look together?

The **art director** thinks the picture is too big on page 4. It is crowding the text. The editor notices that the scene on page 10 takes place in winter. It should be spring. These problems need to be fixed before the art can be colored.

MONTH 1: Author writes a story.

MONTH 2: Author lands an agent.

MONTH 6: Book is accepted for publication.

MONTH 7: Author and editor revise story.

MONTH 8: Book cost is set; publicity decisions are made.

MONTH 12: Illustrator and designer work on the layout.

The editor and art director work together to make sure the book is coming together.

Artist colors the sketches and prepares final art.

MONTH 13 MONTH 14 ING . . . LOADING . . .

A cover design is chosen.

The publisher has told stores when the book will be ready. That date is coming up fast. So many details are left. The team works hard to finish on time.

Proofreaders are combing through every word. They are looking for mistakes. Hold on! The dog's name was *Sam* on page 5. On page 10, it's *Sad*. Spellcheck didn't catch that one.

- MONTH 1: Author writes a story.
- MONTH 2: Author lands an agent.
- MONTH 6: Book is accepted for publication.
- MONTH 7: Author and editor revise story.
- MONTH 8: Book cost is set; publicity decisions are made.
- MONTH 12: Illustrator and designer work on the layout.

Proofreaders carefully read the text. They check for grammar and spelling mistakes.

Artist colors the sketches and prepares final art.

MONTH 13

MONTH 14

MONTH 16

. . . LOADING . . .

A cover design is chosen.

Proofreaders catch mistakes.

A magnifying loupe helps the team closely inspect the printer proofs.

- MONTH 1: Author writes a story.
- MONTH 2: Author lands an agent.
- MONTH 6: Book is accepted for publication.
- MONTH 7: Author and editor revise story.
- MONTH 8: Book cost is set; publicity decisions are made.
- MONTH 12: Illustrator and designer work on the layout.

Printing and Shipping

The mistakes have been fixed. The fixes have been checked. The final color art is ready. At last, the electronic files are finished. They are sent to the printer.

The printer sends back **proofs**. These pages show exactly how the book will print. The team looks over the proofs. This is their very last chance to make changes.

- MONTH 13: A cover design is chosen.
- MONTH 14: Artist colors the sketches and prepares final art.
- MONTH 16: Proofreaders catch mistakes.
- MONTH 17: Printer sends pages for proofing.

ADING . . .

On printing day, machines take over. Workers feed huge sheets of paper into the press. The sheets zip through the rollers. Each roller adds another color to the page.

The wet sheets go through an oven to dry. Then they are chilled. That sets the color, so it will not rub off.

A huge printer has rollers for four ink colors. The inks mix on the paper to make all the colors on each page.

- MONTH 1: Author writes a story.
- MONTH 2: Author lands an agent.
- MONTH 6: Book is accepted for publication.
- MONTH 7: Author and editor revise story.
- MONTH 8: Book cost is set; publicity decisions are made.
- MONTH 12: Illustrator and designer work on the layout.

- MONTH 13: A cover design is chosen.
- MONTH 14: Artist colors the sketches and prepares final art.
- MONTH 16: Proofreaders catch mistakes.
- MONTH 17: Printer sends pages for proofing.
- MONTH 18: **Book is printed.**

- MONTH 1 — Author writes a story.
- MONTH 2 — Author lands an agent.
- MONTH 6 — Book is accepted for publication.
- MONTH 7 — Author and editor revise story.
- MONTH 8 — Book cost is set; publicity decisions are made.
- MONTH 12 — Illustrator and designer work on the layout.

Machines fold the printed paper into pages. The edges are cut to size. Glue or staples bind the pages to the cover. At last, a book rolls off the conveyer line!

A robotic arm stacks the books into boxes. The boxes are loaded onto trucks. They are shipped to stores around the country.

A line of books rolls along to get trimmed. They are almost done.

- MONTH 13 — A cover design is chosen.
- MONTH 14 — Artist colors the sketches and prepares final art.
- MONTH 16 — Proofreaders catch mistakes.
- MONTH 17 — Printer sends pages for proofing.
- MONTH 18 — Book is printed.
- → Book is packaged and shipped.

Read!

The dream has *almost* come true. It needs one last piece—readers!

Little by little, word of the book spreads. A blogger posts a great review. The book wins an award. The author gives a talk at a crowded bookstore. Even better, the author shows up in a classroom, ready to read to eager listeners.

- MONTH 1: Author writes a story.
- MONTH 2: Author lands an agent.
- MONTH 6: Book is accepted for publication.
- MONTH 7: Author and editor revise story.
- MONTH 8: Book cost is set; publicity decisions are made.
- MONTH 12: Illustrator and designer work on the layout.

An author visits a classroom to share her new book with students.

MONTH 13 — A cover design is chosen.

MONTH 14 — Artist colors the sketches and prepares final art.

MONTH 16 — Proofreaders catch mistakes.

MONTH 17 — Printer sends pages for proofing.

MONTH 18 — Book is printed.

Book is packaged and shipped.

GLOSSARY

agent A person who works with an author to sell an author's work to a publisher.

art director A person who is in charge of the pictures, drawings, and layout of a book.

author A person who writes things people will read; authors write things like books, poems, short stories, and news articles.

designer The person who decides how a book will look.

draft An early version of a piece of writing or art.

editor A person whose job it is to make text as good as possible; editors decide if the publisher should produce a book, and then they work with the author to make sure the text is really good.

illustrator A person who draws pictures for a book.

layout The way the words and pictures in a book are placed on the page.

proofs An early versions of a book that the publisher reviews one last time before the book gets printed.

proofreader An editor who looks for mistakes in the text when the book is almost finished.

publicist The person whose job it is to spread news about a new book.

publisher A business that makes and sells books or magazines.

text The words in a book.

READ MORE

Barnett, Mac. *How This Book Was Made: Based on a True Story.* Los Angeles: Disney Hyperion, 2016.

Bram, Elizabeth. *Rufus the Writer.* New York: Schwartz & Wade, 2015.

Malam, John. *Journey of a Book.* Chicago: Heinemann Library, 2013.

Walton, Ruth. *Let's Read a Book: Find out About Books and How They are Made.* Mankato, Minn.: Sea-to-Sea Publications, 2013.

WEBSITES

Eric Carle: How I Create My Pictures

http://www.eric-carle.com/slideshow_collage.html

How Books Are Made / Parts of a Book

https://youtu.be/cu8j7YnunzQ

Scholastic Story Starters

http://www.scholastic.com/teachers/story-starters/

Every effort has been made to ensure that these websites are appropriate for children. However, because of the nature of the Internet, it is impossible to guarantee that these sites will remain active indefinitely or that their contents will not be altered.

INDEX

ABOUT THE AUTHOR

Nadia Higgins has been editing and writing books for 20 years. She has published more than 100 books for kids and teens. Nadia's favorite part of the job is doing research. She uses all kinds of media, from TV shows to podcasts, to find the best facts for her books.